THE
LILY CUPBOARD

by Shulamith Levey Oppenheim • illustrated by Ronald Himler

A TRUMPET CLUB SPECIAL EDITION

Published by The Trumpet Club, Inc.,
a subsidiary of Bantam Doubleday Dell Publishing Group, Inc.,
1540 Broadway, New York, New York 10036.
"A Trumpet Club Special Edition" with the portrayal of a
trumpet and two circles is a registered trademark of
Bantam Doubleday Dell Publishing Group, Inc.

ISBN 0-440-83174-1

This edition published by arrangement with
HarperCollins Publishers.

Printed in Mexico
January 1995
3 5 7 9 10 8 6 4 2
RRR

The paintings are watercolor and gouache on hot-press watercolor paper.

For my grandsons
                    Noah
                    Nathan
                    Micah
and for all children everywhere
                    —S.L.O.

On May 10, 1940, shortly after the beginning of World War II, Holland was invaded by Germany. For five years the Dutch people endured German occupation. Jews in particular were sent to concentration camps, where many died a hideous death. But even in these dark times there were many heroes.

"You know there is a fierce war raging, Miriam." My father is speaking to me quietly. My mother is crying.

"Our tiny country could not hold out against the enemy. Any day now the soldiers will come. That is why you must go into the country. You must be kept out of danger."

"Miriam." My mother takes me in her arms. She smells of silk and lily-of-the-valley.

"Mama," I whisper, "what are you and Papa going to do? Will you be safe?"

"We'll be all right, my dearest girl. Right now you must be kept safe, as Papa said. And before you know it, we will all be together again. The farmer and his wife where you will stay are very kind and very clever. Just do exactly as you are told. Besides"—my mother nearly crushes me against her chest—"it will be much easier for Papa and me to take care of ourselves knowing that you are hidden away in the country."

My mother and I pack one small suitcase. I put in my favorite books.

"Only three," my mother says. "We have to leave room for sweaters and boots."

"You pick them out, Mama. I can't choose." My heart feels like the little stone lantern in our garden, heavy, without a candle.

"What about a doll? You choose." My mother smiles, but I know her heart doesn't have a candle in it either.

"No dolls," I answer. "They have to stay together."

I turn away to hide my tears.

Papa drives me into the country. Tulips and hyacinths and daffodils are blooming everywhere. We stop in front of a low, thatched-roof farmhouse. Fruit trees blossom up against its wall. But it is not my house. The woman has a broad, kind face and wears wooden shoes. But she is not my mama. The man is very tall and smokes a pipe and has a million wrinkles round his eyes. But he is not my papa.

A boy with straw-blond hair and a freckled nose says, "I'm Nello."

"I'm Miriam," I answer. "I don't have a brother."

"I don't have a sister." He grins. He looks funny with his new teeth half in.

My father shakes hands with Nello's parents.
He bends down to give me a hug.
I have to ask him.
"Papa, why am I safer here than with you and Mama?"
"Because this family is not Jewish," he answers very slowly. He kisses my forehead. I try not to let him go, but he is gone.

The cows are black and white and full of milk. Small barges move along the center of the canal. Where is the war?

"Do you know where the war is?" I ask Nello. We're sitting on a bank of grass. I 'm trying not to think of home.

"I don't"—Nello throws a stone into the water—"but Father does. Father says the soldiers will soon be everywhere. That's why you're here."

Nello's parents show me where to hide when the soldiers come. They press a lily painted on the center panel of the cupboard. The cupboard opens. Otherwise it looks just like the wall. I peer inside. It's dark and smells of winter clothes and rubber boots. It makes me cold.

Nello's father is saying, "The warning signal will be whistling 'Frère Jacques.'" He puts his arm around my shoulder. "When you hear it, you must come directly here. After the soldiers have gone, we will knock three times."

"Don't worry, Miriam," Nello's mother says. I like her voice. "Don't be afraid. We'll never be far from you."

That night the feather bed is cozy-warm, and Nello's mother
tucks me in. But it's not my bed. I can't sleep. I can't stop crying,
either. Nello's mother hears me and comes back. She smooths my
curls back from my face.

Next morning Nello's mother says, "I hope you fell asleep, my dear. Of course you miss your parents and your home. Nello would cry if he were not with us. But think how happy your mama and your papa are, knowing you are safe here. Come, I've made some porridge with cream that's thick and clover pink. There's nothing like it. It will make you smile."

"And"—Nello's father puts a basket by my bowl—"I picked some berries long before you woke. They're fresh and ripe and still covered with the morning dew."

He puts the berries one by one on top of the porridge.

"There." He leans back in his chair. "There's a bright-red M for Miriam."

"Thank you." I try to smile. "I want to smile, but..."

Just then Nello jumps from his chair. "Come on." He grabs my hand and pulls me through the door.

Nello's mother calls after us, "The porridge will get cold."

Nello takes me out beyond the kitchen garden near the wood.
The hutch is full of rabbits, big and small.

"Choose one, Miriam." Nello thrusts his hands into the
pockets of his wide blue pants. He's looking very proud. "Go ahead."

A small black rabbit sits apart from all the others, by the wire.
It looks at me. I pick it up. Its fur is like silk. It pushes close against
my chest. I feel its nose twitch cold against my arm.

"I'm going to call you Hendrik." I kiss its ears. "That's my
papa's name."

"Might turn out to be Hendrika." Nello giggles. "My papa says you never know, with rabbits."

"I don't care what he is." I take a long long breath. The ache begins to go away.

"Mama and Papa will be happy that I have a rabbit. They love animals." I kiss Hendrik's nose. "You're mine and I will not let anything happen to you."

The rabbit's eyes are closed. I like his cold nose twitching by my arm.

"You're mine." I kiss his ears again.

"Thank you, Nello." I want to hug him, but Hendrik is in the way. "Thank you. I'll keep him safe. I promise you. If the soldiers come, I'll keep my rabbit safe."

Weeks pass. I spend hours and hours with Hendrik and Nello. Then one day I hear someone whistling "Frère Jacques" just when Hendrik is taking his morning hops. The soldiers must be here!

"Hendrik, come. Come, we have to go!"

Hendrik is nibbling on a bit of green. I creep up slowly, not to frighten him. But just as I reach out, he makes a giant hop into the herbs.

Then I see Nello and his father running toward me. They both are out of breath.

"Miriam, come on!" Nello's face is beet red. "Didn't you hear us whistling?" The freckles on his nose seem very large. "Miriam, the soldiers are only two farms away!"

"I can't go without Hendrik. You know that, Nello. I have to keep him with me. Mama and Papa wouldn't go without him. You know that."

"Never mind the rabbit, Miriam." Nello's father reaches out for me, but I drop onto my knees and scramble into the garden, where I can see my rabbit nibbling on some chives.

"I'm not going into the cupboard without my rabbit! I have to protect him."

"She's not going without her rabbit, Father." Nello's voice is hoarse. "She's named him after her father, and she's going to keep him safe, no matter what."

I look back at Nello's father. He's nodding his head at Nello. Then he scoops up Hendrik and me and we're bounding into the house.

Nello's mother is standing by the cupboard.

"Get in—there's not a second left. Get in, my child, and not a sound!" She doesn't notice Hendrik in my arms.

    This time there is a pillow on the floor. I pull my legs up under me. Hendrik is warm against my chest.

    I wait. I hear heavy footsteps past my wall.

    "It's all right, Hendrik." I comfort him without a sound. His nose is still. I hear the voices of the soldiers harsh and loud. I hear Nello's parents answering, softly and slowly.

I don't know how long we've been waiting, Hendrik and I, but suddenly we hear the three soft knocks…and my lily cupboard opens to the light.

"They've gone." Nello's mother pulls me close.

Nello's father takes a long puff on his pipe.

"Are you all right?" he asks.

"I'm fine, thank you." I smile at Nello. "And so is Hendrik! I told you, Nello, he'd be safe with me." I turn to Nello's mama and papa. "Just the way my parents keep me safe with you."

Families like this one hid Jewish children for five years till the war ended, and saved many lives at the risk of their own.